A Walk Through a
Salt Marsh

by Steven Otfinoski ❦ illustrated by Denny Bond

MODERN CURRICULUM PRESS
Pearson Learning Group

Have you ever seen a salt marsh? On first view, a salt marsh may look like nothing but grass and mud.

But looks can be misleading. A salt marsh is one of nature's most miraculous habitats. It is filled to the brim with life.

Salt marshes are found along coasts. Salt water enters the marsh through a stream or thin channel. The water flows in and out with the tide. At low tide, the marsh is above water. At high tide, it is under water.

What kinds of animals would want to live in such a place?

The answer may surprise you.

Birds and ducks like to build their nests in the soft marsh grass. Large quantities of shellfish and snails move around in the wet mud, eating dead plants and laying eggs. Fish come in with the tide to feed and lay eggs too. All these creatures make the salt marsh one of the richest environments on Earth.

The salt marsh is good for people too.
It is a nursery for many of the fish we eat.
It cleans the sea water and adds rich nutrients.

Salt marshes also help protect us during storms. When there's a big storm or hurricane, large ocean waves come up on the land. The marsh soaks up water like a huge sponge. It fills to the brim with water. This helps stop the flooding of homes farther inland.

Let's take a walk through a salt marsh. Before we begin, make sure you're wearing old shoes and pants. You may get a little muddy!

The first thing you'll notice on this nice fall
day is the salt cord grass. It grows up to nine
feet tall. Its fat roots help hold the marsh soil
together. That stops the soil from washing
away. Its seeds and roots are food for ducks,
geese, and muskrats.

There are many other plants to see here. Some have beautiful flowers. There are the blue blossoms of the sea lavender, the yellow flowers of the seaside goldenrod, and salt spray roses that smell so sweet.

goldenrod

sea lavender

Stop to look at the glasswort. Its heavy stems are filled with water. Some people pick glasswort and add it to salads. They like its salty flavor.

salt spray roses

glasswort

If you look down, you might notice lots of tiny holes in the mud. These are the homes of fiddler crabs.

The male fiddler crab has a huge right claw and a small left claw. It uses the smaller claw to push large quantities of mud into its mouth. Fine bristles around its mouth screen out tiny bits of food from the mud.

Male fiddlers wave their big claws to attract females. The fiddlers also use their big claws when they fight each other.

If the claw breaks in a fight, the crab just grows another one. At the same time, the left claw grows bigger and the new right claw becomes the little one. It's the work of Mother Nature.

Lift up some marsh grass and underneath you'll find another unusual creature. It's the salt marsh snail inside its shiny brown shell.

This tiny snail can only live underwater for about an hour. Twice a day, when the tide rushes in, the snail climbs to the top of the marsh grass, high above the water. When the tide goes out, it climbs back down again.

If you look up, you might see a snowy egret flying gracefully through the blue sky. Its feathers are snow white and its feet are bright yellow.

The egret wades into the marsh water and shakes its foot. This frightens the tiny fish out from the murky bottom. The egret dips its long neck into the water and seizes the fish in its thin bill and eats them. That's lunchtime for the egret.

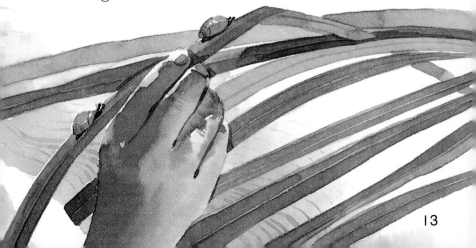

Now look at the marsh flowers. See the beautiful monarch butterflies having a sip of nectar? Their big orange and brown wings are laced with black. The butterflies are only guests in the marsh. They will rest and feed for a short time. Then they will continue their long trip south to Mexico for the winter.

You can see interesting animals here every season of the year. In the winter, black ducks will arrive. In the spring, there will be more to see as other birds and animals return to the marsh.

The salt marsh is a world full of miraculous wonders. It is unfortunate that not everyone sees it that way. Some people see only a worthless swamp.

Over the years, some people have filled salt marshes with garbage or dirt. Then they have built buildings or parking lots there. We need to protect and preserve our salt marshes, not only for the animals, fish, and birds, but for all of us.